George Rooper

The Autobiography of the Late Salmo Salar, esq.

Comprising a narrative of the life, personal adventures, and death of a

Tweed salmon

George Rooper

The Autobiography of the Late Salmo Salar, esq.
Comprising a narrative of the life, personal adventures, and death of a Tweed salmon

ISBN/EAN: 9783744752305

Printed in Europe, USA, Canada, Australia, Japan

Cover: Foto ©Raphael Reischuk / pixelio.de

More available books at **www.hansebooks.com**

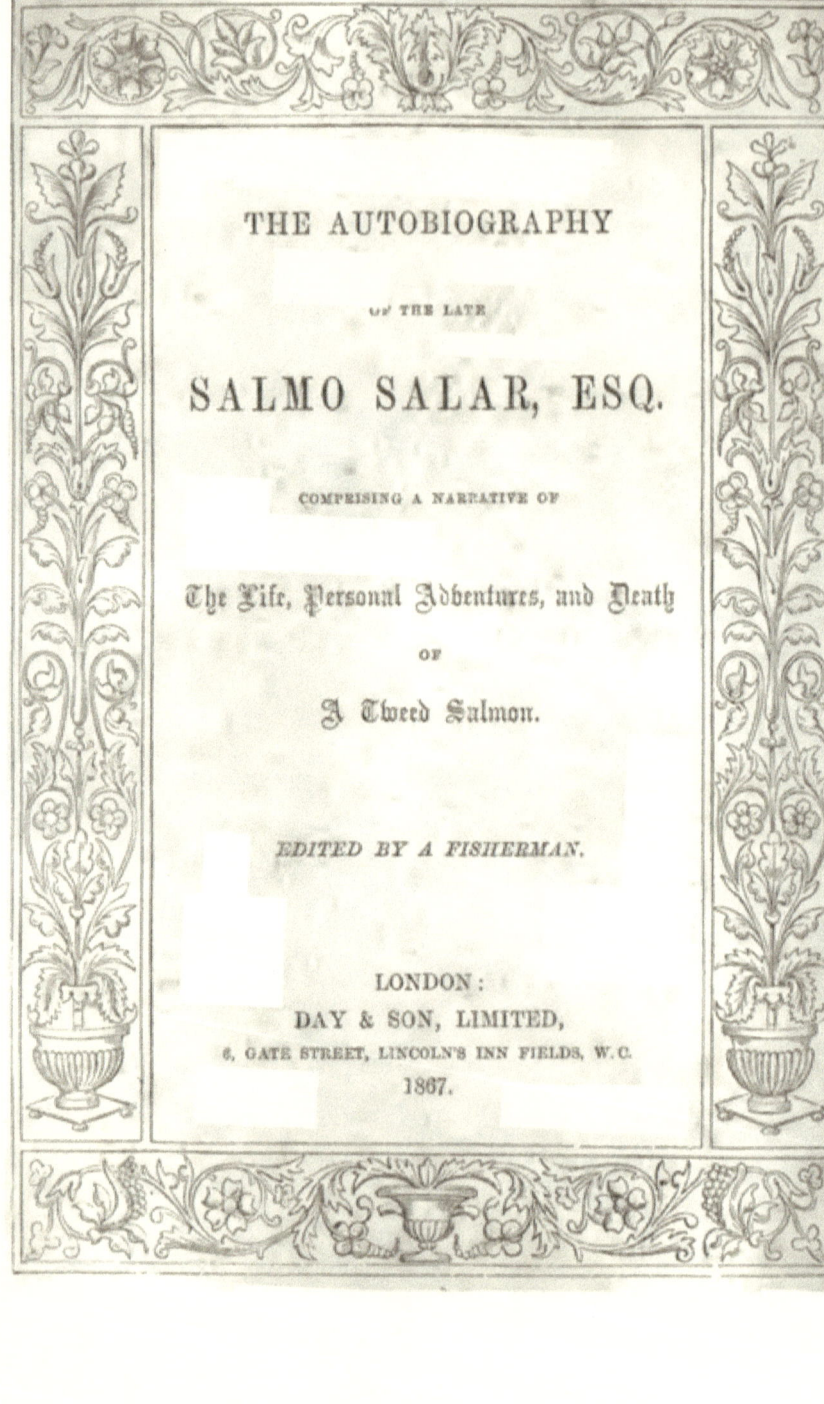

THE AUTOBIOGRAPHY

OF THE LATE

SALMO SALAR, ESQ.

COMPRISING A NARRATIVE OF

The Life, Personal Adventures, and Death

OF

A Tweed Salmon.

EDITED BY A FISHERMAN.

LONDON:

DAY & SON, LIMITED,

6, GATE STREET, LINCOLN'S INN FIELDS, W.C.

1867.

PREFACE.

THE following pages, embodying the result of long experience as a fisherman and careful observation as a lover of Nature, are intended by the Author to convey, in the simple and familiar form of personal narrative, some knowledge of the natural history and habits of that most interesting fish, the SALMON, and some hints as to the mode of capturing him with the artificial fly.

The Author is not vain enough to suppose that he can teach the naturalist or practised fisherman anything he did not know before; but he ventures to hope that, whilst to the tyro some of the facts set forth, and some of the maxims insisted on, may prove both novel and instructive, the incidents recorded and the localities described may awaken in the breast of both naturalist and fisherman pleasant reminiscences of pleasant days passed in that most fascinating of pursuits—Salmon-Fishing. Possibly some of the "dodges" recorded by Salmo Salar may have been practised, successfully or otherwise, upon themselves. The Writer has had experience of each and all.

The "Autobiography" originally appeared in "Macmillan's Magazine." It has since been to some extent remodelled and considerably enlarged; and it is now, by kind permission, with diffidence presented to the public. Should it have the good fortune to meet with approval, it is the intention of the Author to supplement it by a sister sketch of the Hunting Field, under the title of "A Fox's Tale."

THE LATE SALMO SALAR, ESQ.

CHAPTER I.

*I volunteer the story of my life, and commence it before
I was born.*

" I WAS born, or rather———"

"Bless my heart!" said I, somewhat startled,
" *who* are *you?* How did *you* get here ? "

No wonder I was surprised. I had just
quitted the Edinburgh station of the Caledonian
Railway, and, with the accustomed selfish libe-
rality of a young man, I had bribed the guard
to lock me up in a compartment to myself, in
spite of which I now found myself accosted,
without preface or apology, by a queer-looking
old gentleman, dressed in a straw-coloured
paletôt, with a short pipe in his mouth, sitting,
with his legs tucked under him, on the opposite

B

seat to mine, as much at his ease, apparently, as if he had as much right there as I, who had paid two - and - sixpence for the privilege of appropriating six seats to myself.

" Or rather——" he proceeded.

" I really must beg, sir," I began ; but somehow his manner overawed me, as it were, into listening.   I felt like the wedding-guest in the presence of the Ancient Mariner.   He went on in the same tone, without noticing me, or even taking his pipe out of his mouth.

" Or rather, I struggled into existence, for the egg from which I sprang had lain, with countless others, for well-nigh four months previously in one of the tributary streams of the Upper Tweed.   My life, if life it could be called, had hitherto been a dreamy, monotonous, uneventful one, a gleam of sunshine quickening my pulse and increasing the natural yearning I felt for release and liberty, a passing cloud or a chill wind driving me back to somnolency and partial oblivion.   But now the garish beams of the late February sun had called me forth into a new world, and I felt myself, with a proud sense of independence, launched, free from trammels and control, upon that wild waste of waters, henceforth to comprise my habitation and my home.

"Queer little mis-shapen creature that I was! With head and eyes frightfully disproportioned to my size, a little tail, and almost invisible fins, my appearance presented to the unpractised eye rather that of the tadpole, the progeny of the wide-mouthed waddling **frog,** than that of the noble Salmon, the monarch of the waters.

"Still, **Nature, careful of her worthiest** offspring, **had** not neglected the means of preservation **during its** helpless infancy. I found myself furnished, beneath my embryo fins, with a little sack of nutriment, which I felt would sustain me for many days, until my growing strength should enable me to seek the abundant food which the surrounding waters contained, and to escape the numerous enemies that sought to make a prey of me.

"I should say that, when I burst forth from the bed of gravel in which I had so long been buried, very many of my brethren accompanied me, and, as we eyed each other's grotesque forms with astonishment, not unmixed with admiration, we, one and all, urged by the promptings of Nature, scuttled away and hid ourselves, each under some projecting pebble or stone, over which the waters rushed harm-lessly, so far as we were concerned, and in which quiet haven, fed from the sack I have before mentioned, we lay safe, happy, and in full enjoyment of our new life, making obser-vations on the, to us, wide world, which opened to our view."

CHAPTER II.

My infancy.—The perils that attended it.—My enemies.— I moralise, and marvel for what end they were per-mitted to exist.

" LABOUR is the lot not only of man, but of birds, beasts, and fishes. We must all work for our living, and I for one have a natural inclination to swim against the stream; but I own to looking back to this period of my life as one of unmixed happiness. Fed without the trouble of seeking, or even opening my mouth to swallow, my food — sheltered by an over-hanging stone, and lulled by the pleasant ripple of the stream around me—I passed a dreamy, happy existence, without care, or thought, or trouble, and, as the sense of life quickened within me, it brought with it only a deeper sense of enjoyment. 'Where ignorance is bliss, 'tis folly to be wise,' and I may be thankful now that I remained so long in blissful ignorance of the dangers which surrounded me. The power of reflection was not given to me, and, although I saw numbers of my brothers and sisters daily destroyed before my eyes, it never occurred to me as possible that a similar fate might await me. My ignorance, however, was my protection; careless of what was passing around me, I lay under my stone, motionless and fearless, and thus escaped danger until Nature had given me the means of avoiding it.

" When I look back on the number of our enemies, I can only wonder that even one out of our numerous progeny is left to tell the tale. Even the insect tribe was in arms against us; I have seen a huge water-beetle seize an embryo samlet by the throat, and carry it off to devour at his leisure. And the larvæ of sundry insects fed upon us whilst we were in the egg, or newly hatched. More especially that of the dragon-fly—goggle-eyed, mis-shapen, repulsive, its hideous face furnished with a pair of unnaturally elongated eyebrows, and its mouth with sharpest teeth, they would destroy, in the course of a few days, thousands upon thousands of eggs. There was a little brown-coated bird.* with a white waistcoat, the neatest, pleasantest-looking creature imaginable, who would *walk*† deliberately into the stream, and, setting at defiance all laws of gravity, peck away at marine insects, floating morsels of spawn, **and** I greatly fear, though I never actually witnessed the atrocity, little samlets like myself. There was a company of black-headed gulls,‡ who, with loud laughing cry, perpetually hovered over the stream, and, though their professed object was to feed upon the March brown fly which, dead or alive, in countless myriads lined the shore, or covered the face of the waters, never let slip an opportunity of snapping up some little brother or sister that had carelessly left its place of refuge. Then the kingfisher, with rufous breast and glorious mantle of blue,

---

* The Water Ouzel—*Cinclus Aquaticus.*

† Waterton doubts this, but I have seen the operation, times and oft.—*Ed.*

‡ The Laughing Gull—*Larus Ridibundus.*

would dart down like a plummet from his roost, and seize unerringly any little truant which passed within his ken. The appetite of this bird was miraculous; I never saw him satisfied. He would sit for hours on a projecting bough, his body almost perpendicular, his head thrown back between his shoulders; eyeing with an abstracted air the heavens above or the rocks around him, he seemed intent only upon exhibiting the glorious lustre of his plumage, and the brilliant colours with which his azure back was shaded; but let a careless samlet stray beneath him, and in a twinkling his nonchalant attitude was abandoned. With a turn so quick that the eye could scarce follow it, his tail took the place of his head, and, falling rather than flying, he would seize his victim, toss him once into the air, catch him as he fell, head foremost, and swallow him in a second. This manœuvre he would repeat from morning till night; such a greedy insatiable little wretch I never saw! A huge, melancholy heron, too, would station herself knee-deep, near at hand. She was held in terrible awe by me in later days, but at this time I think she despised such 'small deer' as we were; I have seen her, though, kill a rat with a single stroke of her powerful beak, transfix a frog, or swallow an eel in spite of his writhings and struggles, and not unfrequently, to my infinite delight, kill, and carry off to her distant nest, those most hated and destructive foes to our race, our cousins the yellow and bull trout. Yes! our own blood relations are our direst foes, and I have witnessed the destruction, by a hungry old kelt, of fifty of his own progeny for breakfast.

" Artificially bred samlets, confined in large ponds, and daily stuffed with food, escape most of these perils ; but, I think, the system is carried too far. Protected from all danger, the young fry are ignorant of its appearance, and they lose the natural instinct which would otherwise prompt them to avoid it. They are like home-bred boys, who, having been brought up under the surveillance of parents and tutors, only sent forth into the world at an age when other lads, less carefully attended, are fully capable of taking care of themselves, become the easy prey to the sharks and cormorants, and cold blooded, slimy eels, in the shape of usurers and others, whose vocation it is to prey upon them. The grand loss to my race is in the first stage, that of the egg; save these, protect these, hatch these, and leave Nature to do the rest. The nursing ponds, the migratory restrictions, the chopped bullock's liver, and the two years' attendance are useless, and worse than useless, expenses.

"I increased gradually in size; my form developed; the little sack I have alluded to was absorbed, and, with a new-born appetite, I felt was given the power of supplying it. I began to make excursions from my place of refuge, seizing with avidity the minute insects which swarmed in the waters around me, and even rising at times to the surface and seizing some unconscious midge-fly or pre-occupied gnat, that had alighted to drop her eggs on the water. If danger arose, we (for in these excursions I was joined by numberless fry of my own standing) at once rushed for shelter beneath the stones, or sought it in the shallows where our enemies, the great trouts, could not follow us. I remember on one occasion, though it was somewhat later than the period of which I am now treating, how I saved myself, by a desperate manœuvre, from the jaws of a hungry trout. The savage brute singled me out from among all the rest of the shoal, and, hunting me round and round until I was well nigh exhausted, was on the point of making me his prey, when a bold and happy idea occurred to me : springing out of the water, six inches or more upon the dry shingle, I lay gasping and **half** dead with fear, but out of reach of my enemy. The refraction of the water enabled me to see him, though he could not see me ; he beat up and down the spot at which I had disappeared, with much the air of a retriever puppy, when the squirrel he has chased for the first time takes refuge in a tree. His search being in vain, he retired, and I had just strength left to squatter into the water again, and soon regained my accustomed haunt beneath the stone.*

" There seems something very shocking, and contrary to the benevolent design of Nature, that animals so helpless and calculated to enjoy life as we were, should be exposed to these incessant attacks. Why are we not allowed to enjoy life in peace and happiness without fear or danger ?"

* This anecdote was related to me by a lady who witnessed the occurrence, and in whose power of observation, as well as veracity, implicit reliance may be placed.

I broke in here upon the old gentleman's narrative. " Why, sir, did you not tell me me just now that *your* great enjoyment was to devour all the little insects on or beneath the surface of the water that came within your reach?"

" What, sir," said he, testily, " has that to do with the matter? Those miserable animated atoms were, doubtless, created expressly to feed us beings of a nobler order. If you compare a wretched gnat, or a miserable——"

I assured the choleric old gentleman I had no such intention, and begged him to proceed with his interesting narrative.

CHAPTER III.

Having donned my silvery coat, I go forth into the "wide, wide world."—I pass a modest but candid opinion on my own appearance and attributes.

" Time rolled its ceaseless course; days melted into weeks, and weeks into months; upwards of a year* had passed since I—a small, helpless, mis-shapen embryo—had hidden myself under some casual pebble or fragment of a rock. I I was then scarce an inch in length, my body marked with transverse bluish-grey lines, the ' badge of all our tribe,' and my head and eyes altogether out of proportion to my body. I was now some four inches long, trim, well-shaped, and vigorous. Although haunting the waters in which I had first breathed the breath of life, I had long since extended my rambles, and, in company with my brethren, sought the more rapid streams. We rejoiced in our new-born strength to stem the torrent, and vied with one another, whilst poised as hawks in mid-air, in seizing the small insects which were borne along the stream above us. Although there was a sameness in this life, it was not monotonous. We had become sufficiently cognizant of the dangers around us, but, with the buoyancy of youth, we felt more pride in our cleverness in escaping them than gratitude for

---

* My friend S. S. must know best, and it is not for me to contradict him ; but I must say, that for a year old and upwards, he exhibited at this period a very juvenile appearance.—*Ed.*

the escape. Then the changes in the mighty river herself were subjects of perpetual interest. Sometimes stealing along in a quiet, deep channel but a few yards wide, worn through the rock, or between it and the green bank opposite, the spectator would wonder whence the broad expanse of shingle or barren sand had its origin. Little would he wonder, if, after a week's rain, he sought the same spot, when Tweed was coming down in her might, and every tributary stream, transformed for the nonce into a river, swelled the mighty flood. Then, timber trees, sawn wood, dead animals, farming implements, even haystacks, would come floating down, and the very channel of the river would be diverted sometimes never to return to its ancient course. Sad was the havoc occasioned to the embryo spawn ; torn from its bed, it would be carried down the stream, to be devoured by the trout or the eel, or to perish amid the waste of waters.* We felt on these occasions pretty safe. Our principal enemies

---

* This most serious cause of destruction might be greatly lessened by the removal of the spawn from beds exposed to the force of the flood to selected spots unaffected by it, and equally adapted for hatching.

were dispersed: the gulls sought worms in the ploughed-up lands; the kingfisher and the solitary heron flew away to the smaller streams, where the less turbid water permitted them to see their prey. The cold, slimy, cruel eel, alone of all our enemies, was then to be dreaded. Crawling along at the bottom of the water, his flat wicked head pressed against the gravel, so as to escape the force of the stream, the wily beast would insinuate himself into every crevice or corner where a small fish might have taken shelter, or a drowned worm be lodged, and all and either was prey to him. But, as I said, these perils passed lightly over, and were forgotten as soon as passed; 'we had health and we had hope,' and, so that the day passed pleasantly away, we had little care or thought for the morrow.

" A change was, however, to be wrought upon us. I had long observed in my companions, and could not but be conscious within myself, of a striking and beautiful alteration in our external appearance. Without losing the dark blue stripes, the distinctive marks of the salmon tribe, they became gradually coated over, as it were, with bright and silvery scales, as though we had been subjected to the process of electrotyping. I would not be thought vain, but I look back, even now, with feelings **of** pride and delight, at the image memory conjures up of the beautiful appearance we presented. Glancing through the water, we glittered like fire-flies in the air. Our strength had increased in the same ratio as our beauty, and, when I say that our form was nearly as possible that which I now present, I need **hardly say it** was faultless."

"Really, sir!" I interposed, "for a gentleman who disclaims vanity——"

"Sir! I assert that the form of a salmon, fresh run from **the** sea, *is* faultless. Could the vigour he displays, could the strength he possesses, be lodged in any form short of faultless? Could he ascend the cataract—could **he stem** the roaring torrent—could **he**——" The old gentleman was getting into such a state of ebullition that I hastily checked him with a torrent of profuse apologies, not unmixed, I fear with a *soupçon* of flapdoodle, the stuff which Mr. O'Brien informed Peter Simple they feed fools on. Somewhat pacified, he proceeded :—

"With my increasing vigour, a strange feel-

ing of restlessness came over me, a longing
desire to wander forth into some unknown
world of waters. The wide river seemed all
too narrow to contain me; and one glorious
May morning, when the heavy rains which had
fallen on the mountains ' *doon wast* ' had swelled
the river some foot or two, the migratory impulse became irresistible, and, accompanied by
thousands of my companions, actuated by the
same impulse, I dashed away down stream,
seeking ' fresh fields and pastures new.'

"When the prisoner of Chillon looked out
over his dungeon wall upon the waters of Lake
Leman, the fish ' were joyous one and all,' but
never in that still water so joyous as we—
escaping, as it seemed to us now, from a hated
monotonous existence, though Heaven knows
we had been happy enough in it for many a
month—felt, as we dashed along the rolling,
rapid waters of fair Tweed. On! on! we went,
through Boldside Water, and the rapid stream
below it, through Carry Wheel, and that long,
glorious reach of the Pavilion Water, which
stretches from the railway to Melrose Bridge,
through the Wyrlies and the Elm Wheel, and
the still, broad waters that lave the meadows

above Melrose. We leapt out of the water, we raced through the water, we dashed at the flies which settled on the surface ; we would have shouted, but that speech was denied us ; and, exulting in the pride of form and beauty and strength, felt as though fate had no power over us. Alas ! pride goeth before a fall."

CHAPTER IV.

I encounter my first great peril, escape therefrom, and, proceeding on the journey of life, seek the "vast unknown."

" As thus buoyant, elated, and self-confident, I proceeded onwards, I observed a boat, with a young man in it, anchored in strange fashion a little on one side of the main stream down which I was passing. The anchor consisted, in fact, of another individual, older than the occupant of the boat, who, standing in the water as deep as his somewhat long legs would allow, leaned his weight upon the stern of the boat, and so held it fast in its position. I

passed them carelessly, and when but a few
yards in advance, my attention was attracted
to a small, struggling, brown fly, which had
apparently just dropped into the water. Rushing towards it, and rising suddenly to the surface, I greedily seized, and was preparing to
swallow, the delicate morsel ; but scarcely did
it touch my lips when a slight but smart sensation, as of a thorn pricking my mouth, was felt
by me, and I found myself dragged by some
invisible but irresistible force against the
stream, until, half choked, I approached the
boat, into which, by the aid of a light net, I
was instantly lifted. I found myself clasped
by a dreadfully warm hand, and held, in spite
of my struggles, firmly until the hook, attached
to the treacherous fly I had seized, was ex-
tracted, not untenderly, from my wounded jaw.
I was already more than half dead, limp, faint,
and bleeding.

" ' It's just a wee parr beastie,' said the
elder of the two, preparing to slip me into the
water.

" ' It's of no use putting it back,' said the
other ; ' parr or not, it's dead.'

" ' It may dee and be dom'd ; I wash my

hands of it,' was the reply with which my profane friend placed me in the water, carefully enough. I felt sick and helpless; without power to sustain my proper position, I floated, with my back downwards, until I rested against some long floating grass, a few yards from the boat, to which the eddy of the stream had carried me. Although too weak to move, I retained **my** senses, and heard the younger man say to his companion—

" 'Why, John, what made you throw that poor little dead beast into the water again?'

" ' 'Deed,' was the reply, ' yon beastie's just a smolt, an' there's a fine for killing sich like.'

" ' But you killed a parr just now?'

" ' Ay.'

" ' But you call this a parr?'

" ' 'Deed, an' it's the fau't of those who gie the same name to twa different fishes.'

" ' What do you mean?'

" ' A' mean that there's a wee fish ye killed just noo ca'ed " the parr," an' it's a fish of itself,* an' **has** melt an' roe as every ither fish

* I have opened hundreds of the *Burn* Parr, *Salmo Salmulus*, male and female. I have **seen** them **on** their spawning-beds, and taken them out of burns where salmon

has, an' ye'll find it in rivers an' burns, an'
abune waterfalls, an' in mountain tarns, where
no saumon ever yet was seen or could get, an'
it's streekit an' barred all the same as the young
saumon-parr; and it's just the confusion of
ca'ing the twa by the ae name that's raised a'
the fash that's made about the "edentity,"
as they ca' it, of the parr with the young
saumon.'

" 'Then you believe that the parr is not the
young of the salmon?'

" 'If ye ca' the young saumon the parr, the
parr is the young saumon; but there's anither
parr that has a better right to the name, an'
it's a pity that twa fish should be bund to hae
but ae name betwixt them.'

" At this point of the conversation, feeling
myself somewhat recovered from the effects of
my immersion in the uncongenial air, I strug-

never yet ascended, nor could by possibility ascend. I
have baited hooks with the tough little beggars, and released them alive after they had towed a trimmer for six
hours about a loch; the salmon parr being as soft as a pat
of butter, and endowed with about as much power of
sustaining hardships. Doubtless the young salmon is the
parr, but the parr is not *always* the young salmon.—*Ed.*

gled from my resting-place, and, after one or two abortive attempts **at** swimming, which resulted in a circular, aimless movement, I found myself carried out of ear-shot down stream. By the time that I had quite recovered myself, and, with the careless and elastic spirit of youth, had already forgotten the severe lesson I had experienced, I found **myself on the** brink of a precipice, over which, to what unknown depths I could not guess, the great river **was** hurried in ceaseless flow. This was the cauld, **or dam,** that by the supernatural agency of the wondrous wizard, Michael Scott, ' bridled the Tweed with a curb of stone,' just above the beautiful old abbey of Melrose. Pausing for a second **to** collect my energies, instinctively I turned my head up-stream, and, swimming with all my power against it, allowed myself to be carried over the rock, and down into the foaming water below. The shock was much less in reality than in anticipation ; I speedily recovered my senses, and, blithe and free, resumed my downward course. I may mention here, that this manœuvre of swimming **tail** first was constantly practised by us **whenever** the force of the stream was too great to allow of our progressing in the ordinary way. Our movements were eccentric but graceful; darting at intervals ostensibly upwards, but always yielding, and, like the snail in the problem, descending ten feet for every one we ascended. By yielding to the might of the river, we were carried more safely and pleasantly on our destined course.

" Passing the noble ruins of Dryburgh Abbey —scarce, if at all, inferior to those of Melrose —I speedily reached another cauld or dam, and, passing it with equal ease and less fear than the former, swam along by woody Makerstoun through one of the narrow channels called the ' Clippers,' by the magnificent castle of Floors, and, tarrying but to taste the sweet waters of the Teviot, on through Kelso Bridge and Sprouston Dubs, through the Edenmouth and Carham Waters to Coldstream Bridge. In this neighbourhood I escaped, by pure good fortune, a danger that I afterwards learnt proved fatal to thousands—nay, tens of thousands—of my young companions. The stream had apparently divided, and, whilst I followed the course of the right-hand one, the greater number passed down the wider but less rapid left-hand division. Here they speedily encountered a terrific mill-wheel, and, dashing on one side, they found their progress stopped by a small net, which being passed under them, they were landed literally by bushels. My informant, who escaped by passing under the mill-wheel at the imminent risk of being **crushed** to atoms, assured **me** that the bodies of our betrayed brethren were used as manure! And, degrading as the suggestion is, it seems not impossible, for the numbers taken could not be sold or used for food. The water-bailiffs, a useless crew, who, at the time the river chiefly requires protection, usurp the places of the private keepers—connive at or refuse to notice this wholesale destruction, and content themselves by seizing and bringing before the magistrate the wretched urchins who, with a long stick and a long string, a school-boy at one end and the most distant approximation to the semblance of a fly at the other, fill their breeches' pocket with smolts, and run home to boil them for ' daddy's supper.' Doubtless many thousands are destroyed in this way, but what is that when our prolific nature is considered? Every female of our wondrous race lays, on an average, eight thousand eggs!   And, so long as we **have only our** natural enemies to contend with, the **rivers** we affect will be stocked to repletion in spite of all the schoolboys birched betwixt Peebles and Berwick."

CHAPTER V.

The goal is reached.—The "Treasures of the Deep."—I become surfeited with pleasure, and long to re-visit the scenes of my youth.

" You think then, sir," said I, " that the water-bailiffs are useless ? "

" By no means," said he, in a more argumentative and less dictatorial tone than he had hitherto used; " but they should be supplemental to, and not in the place of, the ' fishermen ' or private keepers. These men know every pool, and rock, and haunt of a fish, spawning or otherwise, on their respective waters. **They are** directly interested in the increase of the fish, and they generally know and are *not* connected with the poachers. Yet **on a certain day, as a rule, the keepers,** one or more of whom are attached to each water, are *functi officiis*, and their places supplied by water-bailiffs, to one of whom is frequently entrusted three or four miles of river, and who is somehow invariably at the farthest part of the beat, whilst his kinsmen, and possibly former comrades, are stopping the ascending or ' leistering ' the spawning fish."

I have always doubted in my own mind whether the above lucubrations emanated in reality from my strange companion, or whether they were not in fact the embodiment of my own dreamy notions: for, truth to say, my friend had become somewhat prosy, and an " exposition of sleep " had come over me. I roused myself, however, and listened with marked attention as he proceeded in his natural tone :—

" At last, then, we had attained the goal of our hopes, the unknown object of our yearning aspirations ; and never were wishful anticipations—offspring of the promptings of Nature— more abundantly satisfied. Not only did the novel element in which we found ourselves— for so unlike was it to that which we had hitherto inhabited, it might properly be so called—brace and invigorate our frames, rendering us keenly sensible of the delightful sensation of wandering at will, through what seemed to us boundless space; but the waters absolutely teemed with life,—marine insects and molluscs, shrimps and prawns, young crabs and lobsters, sea-worms, embryo creatures of lower organization in millions, all destined doubtless for our sustenance and delectation, and for the gratifying (satisfying seemed out of the question) our appetite, which ' grew with what it fed on.'   And we grew too; how could we otherwise, consuming as we did almost our own weight daily of the most nutritious and **palatable** food ?

" I have heard wonder expressed that so small a fish as the smolt should, in a few short months, increase from the weight of three or four ounces to that of frequently twice as many pounds.   But where is the wonder ?   My mother, who was murdered on the spawning beds **before** half her eggs had been deposited, weighed twenty pounds; the noble kipper, her companion, half as much again.   What would be the weight at more than two years old of a dog, offspring of parents such sizes ?   And was ever puppy fed as we were fed? No! *Fortes creantur fortibus.* Large animals and large fishes produce large offspring, and when I left the sea and again ascended my native Tweed in July, I weighed nearly seven pounds.* But I anticipate.

" Although the world of waters was all before us where to choose, we never **of** our own accord wandered far away from the land. Coasting along we hugged the shore, and thereby not only secured a greater abundance of food, but escaped many dangers to which those who were driven by accident or fear away into the unknown depths of remoter waters were exposed. **True,** danger even in the humble path we had chosen for ourselves met us in

---

* A suggestion offers itself here, which I put forward with great diffidence. Instead of putting back the under-sized fish, the necessity for which is now so strongly advocated, suppose the angler were occasionally to return those monsters of the deep whose capture and dimensions we occasionally find recorded in the *Field* and other papers devoted to sporting matters. Would not the probable result be an increase in the *size* of the fish? **After** all, small fry are pleasant eating, and exist in such numbers that the effect of rod-fishing upon them is absolutely inappreciable.

every turn. Dog-fish and cod-fish, and por-
poises, and seals, and otters preyed upon us
remorselessly, but the numbers of the four first,
at least, were greatly increased as we increased
our distance from the shore; besides which, we
lost those landmarks which gave us confidence
that we should one day be enabled to retrace
our steps, and saved us from the bewildering
sensation of being utterly lost. Few fish, once
driven out to sea, ever returned to our company; they were devoured, or perished from
want of proper food, or, if haply they reached
some unknown shore, wandered listlessly and
helplessly along it, seeking a stream or river
suitable to their wants, and, finding none,
perished miserably.

" Great indeed is the wickedness and heavy
the responsibility of that greedy, selfish class—
thank Heaven! now at last a limited one—
which, having acquired in some incomprehen-
sible manner the legal right of privately
destroying what ought to have been the most
cherished, as it is the most valuable, public
property, planted those accursed engines, the
stake-nets, along the coast and in the tideways
known as the highways most frequented by our

persecuted race. Nor is the fatal result that of
chance only. As the shoal of salmon and grilse
feel their way along shore, they run against the
guide-net, stretching far away into the sea.
Turning to avoid the danger seaward, they are
exposed to the attacks of ravenous hakes and
dog-fish, approaching **in size to** sharks; these,
with the seals, watch the entrance to **the** nets
in murderous numbers, having learnt by experience the rich banquet afforded by the
terrified fugitives.

" However, these and many other dangers,
which in the course of twelve months left
scarcely one **in** five hundred of my original
companions alive, affected such of us as escaped
no more **than the** unknown perils of our child-
hood. ' Heaven from all creatures hides the
book of fate.' **My** life was passed in one continued dream of sensual enjoyment.

" But all such pleasures, even to **the** brute
creation, are of short duration. I had for some
little **time** become aware of a feeling of satiety,
a desire for change; and it was, I think, about
the middle of June that this feeling **heightened**
into an impulse, strong as that which, in May of
the previous year, had driven me down into the

sea. As to Lord Lovel, 'a longing wish came over my mind' to revisit my early haunts, and to taste again that sweet fresh water I had so gladly left. Besides, whilst wandering through the waving groves of sea-weed in search of **my** prey, certain sea-lice had detached themselves from their sapless stems, to browse upon my 'fair pasture.' They swarmed upon my gills, and other parts of my body, to my great annoyance. Instinct told me that these creatures could not exist in fresh water; so, in company with a few stragglers, the remnants of my early companions, and many elder fish, I turned my head, and resolutely commenced my homeward journey."

CHAPTER VI.

I return.—My reception.—My second great peril.

" ALTHOUGH the time spent in the sea was really considerable, and the experience acquired appeared to our youthful imaginations illimitable, the actual distance passed in our wanderings was not great, and a few days found us at the broad estuary into which fair Tweed empties herself.

Here, after tarrying a short time to accustom our palates to the change from salt to fresh water, and impelled by the sweet taste of an unusual flow of the latter, we ran at once into the mouth of the river, prepared to ascend with the flowing tide of that night. Little indeed did we calculate upon the destructive power of men, whose living was our death. We had collected, as I said, by hundreds, still in the sea, but close to the mouth of the river. Suddenly a boat, manned by two stout rowers, put off, and, whilst they rowed quickly round us, the third paid off an immense net of apparently endless length, and deep enough to sweep the bottom. So rapidly was this effected, that, notwithstanding a strong feeling of imminent danger, we found ourselves surrounded, and, the two ends of the net being joined on the shore, entrapped and confined within a circle becoming, as it was hauled in, gradually of smaller dimensions. In vain, swimming wildly about and around, we sought some outlet of escape—there was none; slowly, but

surely, the mighty circle lessened and still
lessened, until we found ourselves dragged to
the very shore, and there, heaped on one
another, we lay, a mass of helpless, struggling
fish, gasping, flapping, choking, suffocating,
rolling one over another, and exhausting our
little remaining strength in futile jumps, or vain
endeavours to hide ourselves beneath the
doomed mass of the victims. Already the dull,
heavy thud of the short club, used by the
fishermen to despatch those fish that came
readiest to hand, sounded in our ears; already
hope had given way to despair, and I, like the
rest, felt with the hope the desire of life to
perish; when a cry arose among our captors
that the net was breaking! Such indeed was
the fact; the net had been pulled somewhat
too high upon the shore, and the vast weight
of more than three hundred fish, aided by the
struggles of some of the heaviest, broke the
meshes, and in a moment we were free! Many
of my companions were nevertheless seized and
killed; but by far the greater number, myself
included, rushed through the wide opening, and
dashed back again to the friendly sea we had
so lately left. What became of my companions

I know not,—many doubtless were lost, many devoured: for myself, I lingered sadly about the spot, and should have in all probability shared the latter fate, but that I was accosted by a female of my own race, bright and beautiful, but twice my size and age. She told me she was seeking the spawning-beds above, and I, as youth ever does, felt an instinctive love and veneration for one so much older and grander than myself. She told me of the dangers she had escaped, almost by a miracle, the year before; how, after being twice all but taken in the drag-nets, from which I had just escaped, she had entered the river; how for some miles as she ascended, when her back or that of her larger companion was seen above the surface of the shallow water, there had been a cry of 'Fash! Fash!' and then a net had been hastily dragged across her path, whilst another was stretched below to prevent her return; how men with loud shouts or splashings of the water had driven the devoted fish into the toils before them; how at each projecting rock, forming still water where the struggling fish might rest, a net was placed; *

* These nets are now prohibited by law.

how the deep pools affording a more permanent **harbour were** dragged ; and how, when at last the shallow spawning-beds were attained, many of her race were ' gaffed ' for the sake of the spawn within them.   Such was the fate of **the** baggit from which I sprang, some particulars of which I learnt in after-times.   I may as well relate them now."

———

CHAPTER VII.

The Baillie's misadventure in search of "Saumon Roe."— Mode of fishing with that prohibited bait.

" I was lying listlessly one day in summer thirty feet beneath the surface, beyond the influence of the rapid stream above, in the fathomless pool called The Pot, some half-mile below Merton Bridge, a boat, kept in its place by two light oars, floating above me, when the fragments of a conversation reached my ears, which by degrees absorbed my attention.   A river-keeper was detailing to his employer the circumstances connected with the capturing of a poacher.

" ' Ay, sir,' he said, ' but that saumon-roe is a sair temptation; mony a guid mon has been beguiled by it. A' ken ane, a baillie; a' took him mysel'.'

" ' How came that? Tell us all about it,' was the reply.

" ' A' was watching, mebbe six months syne, up in the Pavilion Water; the fish were thranging sair upon the spawning-beds, and weel a' kent they were thrang on the bank abune the Whirlies. A' was hidden in the wee brae just abune the brig, and a' hadna' been there mebbe twa hour, when a' see a mon come daintily alang. Looking carefully this way an' that, an' seeing naebody, he just out wi' the gaff, an', screwing it on to the end of his walking-stick, stepped lightly into the water. It wouldna' be mickle abune his knee, an' the back fin o' mair than ae great fish was plain to be seen on the bank before him. 'Deed, but he wasted little time in selection, an' varra little ceremony he treated 'em with. In a second the gaff was in a puir half-spawned beastie, an', lugging her ashore, he started aff het foot towards Melrose. A' up an' after him, an' for a weighty mon he made mickle running. When he saw me he dropped the fish, but no' stopping to pick it up, a' just kept on under the railway brig, down the meadows, by Ailwand Foot, under Melrose Brig, an' there, as he was creeping up the steep bank, a' grippit hold of him ahint; a' grippit hard, an' he turned and said, " Sandy, lad! dinna grip sae hard; ye'll rive ma breeks." " Ay, Baillie," said I, " is that you? How cam' ye to do it?" And he said quite solemn-like, " Sandy!" he said, " It was neether the need nor the greed, but *joost the saumon-roe!*" " Ech, Baillie," a' said, " a' wadna' have believed it of ye, but it will be dear saumon-roe to ye." And sae it proved, for he was fined five pund, and ither harm cam' of it.'

" ' And served him right,' said his companion; ' a man ought to be hanged who kills a spawning fish on its bed. Why! the very Jews under divine command spared the sitting bird, the nursing mother; and what is the value of a flavourless bird laying half-a-dozen eggs at most, to that of the noble salmon which lays eight thousand!'

" ' 'Deed, ye speak true, sir,' said the other voice ; ' an' its aye a strange thing to me, that ony ca'ing themselves sportsmen can condescend to fish wi' roe. It's just no sport ava, an' the best trouts that are killed, though the biggest in the haill river, are no worth the killing.'

" ' Indeed, I believe you ; but I never saw the operation of fishing with roe. How is it performed ? '

" ' Aweel, ye require neither rod, nor line, nor gut, nor reel, nor onything but just a strong stick—a stake out of the hedge is about as guid as anither—an' a bit of cord, no matter how thick, an' a heuk with a bittock of lead to sink her, an' a lump of roe as muckle mebbe as a marley is put intil it ; an' ye tak' the highest flood and the darkest water, an' ye stan' on the bank, an' the spent trout that have spawned, ye ken, seek the still waters close in shore, an' they're varra empty and hungry belike, an', when ye feel they swallow the roe, ye just fling 'em ower your head ; an' a' the best trout in Tweed are caught that way.'

" ' By Jove ! ' said his companion, ' your friend, the baillie, deserved a ducking for his

snobbishness, as well as a fine for his wickedness! I wish I had the power, and I'd make
it felony to fish with salmon-roe."

"Sinking down to the quiet depths below,
and pondering upon what I had heard, I fully
concurred in the sentence last uttered, on
general as well as selfish grounds."*

CHAPTER VIII.

The ascent of the river.—I find again to my cost that
  "all is not gold that glitters," and afford a practical
  illustration of "the biter bitten."—My third great
  peril.

"DANGERS, fears, and perils forgotten, the next
morning found my companion and myself again

---

* There are those who think that the common trout, on
account of the injury he does to the salmon-roe, should be,
if possible, annihilated. I differ ; but, with that object in
view, no more efficient instrument exists than angling in
spring with roe. After all, trout only eat that portion of
spawn which, from two females in succession occupying the
same spawning-bed or other causes, has been dislodged and
floats down the stream, and which under any circumstances
must be lost. The insidious attacks of the dragon-fly larvæ
are a million times more destructive, and, what is worse,
impossible to be guarded against.

at the mouth of the river. The scarce-ebbing
tide brought with it the smell and taste of a
freshet, the result of the last night's rain, and
we stemmed the retreating tide more boldly as
we felt the assurance of good swimming-water
above.

" It was Saturday morning; from that day
to Monday the river is free; so for thirty hours
at least our persecutors were restrained from
crying ' Havoc ' upon our devoted race. No
net, no boat, stopped our way; we swam
joyously up stream, and by noon that day had
passed the well-remembered Norham Bridge.
Here we met a little crowd of frightened fish,
returning to the sea, dismayed and disheartened,
as well they might be. This sparse band, scarce
half a score in number, were all that remained
of some five hundred noble fish who had attempted the passage but the day before. They
had escaped the long sea-nets, and the more
deadly drags used in the river; they had been
hunted in the shallows, and pelted in the streams,
and when they might fairly hope for rest and
safety, they had found themselves debarred
from the goal they sought, by a long, deep,
heavy net fastened right across the stream,

sunk a little below the water, and intended to
keep the fish from passing upwards during the
short period from Saturday to Monday, when
net-fishing ostensibly ceases, until they could
legally be dragged out of the pool on Monday
morning. They urged us to return,* and seek
the comparative safety of the sea, swarming as
it did with our natural enemies, in preference
to placing ourselves within the power of those
short-sighted, unprincipled scoundrels who dis-
grace the name of fisherman ! Had I been
unsupported, my natural timidity, enhanced by
the remembrance of the dangers I had gone
through, would have induced me to accompany
them, but my more experienced and bolder
companion overruled their counsel. She told
them how, by swimming on the surface of the
water, instead of the bed of the river, on which
to escape the force of the stream our course
had hitherto been held, we should escape the
danger, and how essential it was to our health,
and the preservation of our race, that the upper

---

* Running fish, especially grilse, are frequently turned
back by meeting others which, having been scared by the
nets, are again returning to the sea, thus affording a double
chance of capture to their vigilant enemies.

waters, where alone fitting spawning-beds could be found, should be reached ; she pointed out how even yet the sea-lice clung to our gills and bodies, and promised us that twenty-four hours' sojourn in the fresh water would relieve us from each one : finally, taunting us with the timidity evidenced by going back after daring so much and advancing so far, she succeeded in persuading us to risk all chances and follow her lead. For myself, I dashed recklessly after her over the net of which we had already taken stock, as we advanced towards it. Many of our companions followed, and a few hours brought us, without further let or hindrance, to the Cauld Pool, below the well-remembered ruins of Dryburgh Abbey, where all that is mortal of the great poet and novelist of Scotland lies interred. Here, taking advantage of the comparatively still water behind a large submerged rock, we rested motionless and silent, and though 'we, like mortals, never sleep,' enjoyed that perfect rest which cessation from labour, and the total oblivion from cares and troubles, ever bring with **them**.

"This, and a portion of the following day. were thus serenely spent. The sea-lice which had clung to our scales, unable to exist in the fresh water, **had** dropped off, and no care or trouble was present. A restless feeling **had,** indeed, arisen within me, and I was on the point of suggesting to my companions a movement higher and still higher up the stream, when my attention was attracted by what appeared to me a familiar object—a shrimp or prawn, or some other small object of the ocean so lately quitted, and which had furnished me with many a bountiful meal. It floated gently over my head, not over bright in colour, but showy, and its hues, which were dispersed uniformly over its body, blended together, and formed one harmonious whole. Its movements **were** short and rapid, such as are those of the insects—'Crustaceæ,' I think, **is** the proper term—I have referred to, and it seemed to be striving, with doubtful result, to stem the somewhat rapid stream. What induced me I cannot say: I was not hungry; indeed, I had felt no desire to eat since I entered the fresh water; I was hardly in the mood for play, for I felt **that the serious** business of life was before me; but, impelled by some unaccountable impulse, I rose from my resting-place, and

attempted to seize it in my mouth. The motion
was rapid, but still too slow to be effectual;
the creature vanished ere my lips could close
on it. Whilst turning slowly round to seek
my former station—somewhat sulkily, too, for
the object I had failed to attain had, in con-
sequence, acquired a value it had not previously
possessed—I heard a voice say,—

"'Ay, but that was a bonny grilse! Ay,
but it was a grand rise he made, too! Ye
were ower quick in striking.'

"'I think I was,' was the reply, 'but we'll
try again.'

"'Bide a wee, sir; bide a wee; give him
time to return to his old station before you
show him the flee again.'

"Utterly unconscious of the meaning of
these words, and in no respect connecting them
with myself or my doings, I saw with some
surprise, not unmixed with pleasure, the
little jerking figure again passing within three
feet of my nose. There was a band of silver
round its throat that excited my cupidity,
and I was, moreover, somewhat nettled
at the failure of my previous attempt to
seize it. Without a moment's pause, I dashed

at it, and, seizing the bright wings between my
lips, was prepared, at least, to carry it down
with me, to be swallowed or not, as might
happen; when, to my amazement and alarm,
ere I could as much as turn away after my
spring, the creature snatched itself from out
my very jaws, and vanished as it had previously
done. Sulky and annoyed, I sought again my
resting-place, and again I heard the same voice
which had before spoken,—

"'Deed, sir, ye were just ower hasty again;
ye dinna let the fash tak' a grip of the flee
before you snatch it out of his mouth.'

"'Never mind, Sandy; we'll try again.'

"'A'm thinking I'll just change the flee;
mebbe he's seen ower muckle of this ane.'

"Read from the light of after-experience,
these words were plain enough; but, young
and inexperienced as I was, they conveyed no
meaning, no warning, and it can hardly be
wondered at that, tantalized as I had been,
no sooner did I see a creature similar in form
and habit to the other, but somewhat larger
and brighter, apparently striving to stem the
stream a little above me, than, again dashing
at it, I seized it firmly in my teeth, and,

turning round, was going back to my lair,
when I felt a sharp, smarting pain, a convulsive shock shook my frame, and I found myself
madly struggling against some great, unknown,
invisible power, which controlled my will, and,
for a time at least, rendered me helpless,
almost hopeless.

" Willing to realize the worst, and anxious
to learn something certain respecting my con-
dition, I rushed upwards, and, jumping high
in the air, saw two men standing on the
bank, with whose movements, with reference
to my own position, I had no difficulty in
tracing the connexion. The one with a long
rod in his hand, the line from which restrained
and controlled me, stood motionless; whilst
the other, with a horrible hook attached to
the end of a stick in his hand, seemed to be
aiding and advising him.

" ' Canny, lad,' I heard him say ; ' canny,
noo ; he is but light heukit ; I ken by his
jumping. Canny, noo ; he's just a fresh-run
grilse, an' his mouth unco saft.'

" I had heard enough ; and by this time
my terror had somewhat abated, and my
natural energy returned in aid of the strength

with which I was gifted. No longer coursing about the pool with aimless rapidity, or wasting my strength in fruitless jumps, I dropped back gradually into the deep pool behind, and, **sinking** to the bottom, lay motionless behind the big rock I had so lately quitted. My companion **kept** ever beside me, and, though she could render no assistance, her presence was an aid and consolation to me, and I **felt** cooler and stronger for her sympathy. Aided by the weight of water above me, I defied the power still exercised by my persecutor to move **me.** I felt but little pain, and, but for the choking sensation occasioned by the interference of the free passage of water through my gills, little annoyance; and it was only on observing a huge stone thrown for the purpose of dislodging me, descending directly upon my head, that I started from my lair. Rushing wildly away, my escape was brought about by the very means intended for my destruction. Impeded by the line, my movement was slow, and the stone, barely missing me, fell upon the line itself, released the hook from the slight hold it had in my mouth, and I felt that I was free ! Joyous, exulting in my deliverance, I again sought the

surface, and, as I jumped two or three times
out of the water, I had the satisfaction of **ob-**
serving visible marks of disappointment and
regret on the countenances of my friends on
shore. The one stood with his rod straight
upwards, his line floating down the stream,
himself in the precise attitude in which he had
maintained that dead, strong pull against me,
which, by exhausting my strength, had so
nearly proved fatal; the other was apparently
solacing himself with a pinch of snuff, and the
only words **I heard** him utter were,—

"'Ay, but that was a bonny grilse! Deil
tak' the stane!'"

CHAPTER IX.

I foregather with a kelt, **whose** gallant struggle **and**
ultimate capture **I witness.**

"THE Cauld Pool, **so** lately **a** pleasant haven of
rest, was no longer an abiding-place for **me.**
The dread and terror I had endured were asso-
ciated with every **rock** and **stone about me;**
and, had I stayed there **for a month** to come, I
am certain that **no gaud,** however cunningly

devised, would have tempted me so much as to look at it. The freshèt, however, still continued; there was good swimming-water, and that very night, my faithful companion by my side, I ascended the heavy fall which descended the 'cauld' or dam, and proceeded onwards towards those faintly but dearly remembered scenes of my early youth, the waters of Upper Tweed.

" I may here correct a very common error as to the manner in which we salmon ascend a rapid. In many pictures, in many books, we are represented as leaping over a rapid some fifteen or twenty feet in height. This is simply absurd. Excepting in the exuberance of spirits, occasioned by escape from danger, the attempt to escape that danger, or under the peculiar influence caused by a change in the weight of the atmosphere, we never *jump*: we *swim* upwards, and the effort carries us beyond the surface high into the air; we *swim* up a rapid, and what appears like a jump is nothing more than the abortive result of a misdirected effort; an attempt, in fact, to swim in a perpendicular direction up a stream, which descends more or less horizontally.

" One or two failures occurred, but with little
difficulty we surmounted the obstacle, and,
passing rapidly onwards by the low green
meadows and woody banks above Melrose, we
made no further pause till we reached that long
extent of unrivalled water, where may still be
seen the foundations of the old bridge, the gate
of which, in the days when ' the Monastery '
was still entire, was kept by the churlish Peter,
the bridgeward. Here, again, choosing our
station behind a projecting stone, we rested;
and, whilst many of our companions passed
onwards, a considerable number, and those of
a large size, took up their position around us.
Indeed, the place was, in every respect, satis-
factory, and adapted to our requirements.
Shelving gradually from the southern side, the
force of the stream increased proportionately
with its depth, so that, with the least trouble,
we could seek such depth and strength of
water as suited our tastes for the time : excepting a few large stones, behind which we usually
lay, the bottom of the stream was perfectly
level; and, as the river made a considerable
angle on the opposite side, beneath the steep,
wood-crowned bank, we could at any time bask

in the sun, or exchange its sultry beams for the
cool shadow beyond.

" In addition to the companions of our voy-
age, and many others who had previously a-
scended with the same object—to deposit their
spawn on the gravelly beds, so common in the
upper waters—our pool contained a large number of kelts :* fish, that is, which during the
preceding winter and early spring had successfully deposited their spawn, and were now
sinking downwards **by** easy stages towards
that land, if I may use an Irishism, of plenty,
the sea. These kelts were the jolliest of fish ;
they seemed like married men escaped for a
short period from the cares of a family, and the
troubles of housekeeping. They ate minnows,
and parr, and the late samlets of the previous

---

* I constantly observe in that excellent paper, the *Field*,
pungent gibes directed against the slayer of the kelt. In
the same paper, too, I occasionally observe diatribes upon
battue-shooting, which **is** likened **to** slaying cocks and hens
in a farmyard. Now, I am no friend to over-preserving,
and fully admit that battue-shooting may be carried too far ;
but the man who can stand at a cross-ride and toss five out
of six rocketing pheasants dead ten yards behind him, **or**
can kill a " weel mendit" kelt in Tweed, in the month of
May, take my word for it, is no muff !

year, and water insects, and worms, and slugs,
and, in fact, whatever came uppermost. Though
thin and emaciated when they left the spawning beds, good cheer told upon them, and I
have rarely seen a handsomer specimen of our
race than a grand eighteen-pound kelt, with
whom I struck up a passing acquaintance as
we sheltered behind the same stone in the Brig
End Pool. He was, perhaps, a trifle longer in
proportion to his depth than a fresh-run fish;
his back had a bluish tinge, and he was less
thick about the tail; but the scales beneath
were of silvery white; he was altogether
well-proportioned and well-favoured; and his
strength was evidenced by the ease with which
he poised himself, like a bird in the air, even in
the rapid part of the stream. What fun it
must be, thought I, to be hungry! as I saw
him dash playfully upwards at a gaudy-winged
butterfly which, after hovering a moment above
us, had dropped exhausted into the stream,
and was now, despite his struggles, manifestly
drowning. I had seen my friend the day
before, when the water was somewhat muddy,
absolutely gorge himself upon dead worms, and
other not over-delicate *débris*, that floated down

the stream. The butterfly was more after my own taste, and, as he rose at the painted fly, he rose in my estimation. But what is this? Scarcely had he, with a sweep of his mighty tail, reached the surface, when he descended again, rushing by me in evident terror and alarm, and seeking, with a rapid but rather constrained motion, the dark depths below. The facts of the case were apparent to me instantly. My poor friend, in the buoyancy of his spirits, had seized, more in playfulness than in greed, the treacherous imitation of a fly, cast by one of the deadliest foes to our race on Tweed. No hope of release from a friendly misdirected stone was here; if a stone were thrown by him it might startle, but never loose, the fish; and, confident in the strength of his tackle and the delicacy of his touch, little did the fisher heed the poor kelt's attempt at sulking. Not, as in my case, was the strain upwards, giving me the advantage of the whole weight of water to increase the resistance, but sideways the force was exerted, at an angle which deprived the devoted fish of all help from that source. Indeed, the run of the stream was in the direction of the slow, strong, steady pull, persistently kept up, and to which at first slowly, but eventually with a rush, like that of a hawk through the air, the kelt was constrained to yield. Dashing up stream, with a velocity still comparable to that of the bird, he sought the rough pass above the railway bridge, where haply he might cut the envious line against the sharp edges of the rocks, or rub the cruel hook from the jaw in which it was too securely fixed; but this was not allowed. The strong, pliant rod was in no tyro's hand, and the maddest efforts of the fish were controlled by a power which, though felt to be irresistible, could never be measured or met by opposed strength. In vain, rushing upwards, did the poor animal dash three feet from the surface of the water into the thin air, hoping in his descent to fall upon the line, and so disengage the biting hook; in vain, I say, for rod, and eye, and line, and hand seemed guided by one impulse alone, and that derived from the struggling fish. As he jumped, the hand yielded, the rod bent, the strain of the line loosened, and the quiet eye twinkled with exultation, as, gaining nothing by the exhausting effort, the poor fish sought again his native element. Weakened and failing, unable to drag the weighty line against the rapid stream, the fish now turned his head downwards, and with an imitation, rather than the reality, of strength, dashed away at his former pace. But swimming down stream, with a hook in one's mouth, is a game that cannot be long played. Breathing, as fishes breathe, becomes impossible; and with pain I speedily beheld my poor acquaintance turn on his back, and approach, with no will of his own, the low shelving bank of shingle, where the shallow water left half his huge body exposed. A large net was passed under him, and whilst, as being dragged ashore, the exulting 'whoo whoop!' of his captor rang in my ears, I naturally concluded that I had seen the last of my gallant, handsome, ill-fated friend. Such, however, was not the case; and the conversation that reached me before he was returned to the water, as to my great surprise he was, explained the cause of his good fortune.

CHAPTER X.

"Thou rash intruding fool! I took thee for thy betters."
HAMLET.

" ' Hurrah! hurrah! A clean fish at last! **And what a beauty!** What do you think of *that?*'

" 'Hoot! It's no fash ava! It's just a kelt beastie.'

" 'A kelt! Why, now I look at it, it is a kelt; but it is a grand fish, and the sport it showed **first-rate.**'

" 'And what for no'? A fish that's fattened in the river, wi' guid, wholesome food, is just as strong as ony fattened in the sea, an' it kens, mind ye, every hole, and stream, and rock in the pool, an' it's no' sae frightened at the bank's side as a fash fresh-run from the sea, where there **is no bound** on ony side.'

" 'And about the eating?'

" 'Weel, I'll no' say that the eating is sae guid as a clean fresh-run saumon: 'deed, there's naething in nature can beat that; the

fash caught in the nets are no' to be compared
to it; but it's guid, wholesome food for a' that,
an' dainty eneuch. I was up to London ten
years syne to gie evidence, as they ca' it,
anent saumon and sich like, an' ech! the
evidence I heard given! There was ae lad swore
that *his* fish were bred in the sea, an' had no
necessity to come to the rivers at a'! There
was anither swore that it was the Saturday's
slap that destroyed the fish, for it just allowed
those who would have returned to the sea,
there to spawn in safety, to gae up the river
to be kilt by the poacher! I saw on the stalls
of the fishmongers, as ye ca' them, mony mair
kelts than clean fish; an', though they were a
thought paler in colour, an', I kenned weel,
varra inferior in taste, they seemed to sell
t'ane as well as the ither.'

"'Then you think kelts ought to be killed?'

"'Hoo,' not at a'! But a kelt that is fit to
be kilt an' eaten should be kilt an' eaten.
What for no'? Ye'll tak' mebbe twal or
aughteen fish in a morning, an', out of them
a', twa or four, mebbe, are weel mendit. A'd
gie *them* a tap on the head, an' they're just the
fish that gie the greatest sport, an' mony ane

dees from exhaustion when putten back into the river. The rest might swim away an' be thankful, an', if some of them dee, what are they after a' but single fish ?'

"Whilst speaking, my friend had carefully disengaged the hook from the gasping fish, and, with one hand below its body beneath the water, and the other grasping its tail, had launched him, as it were, into the deep pool. As it felt itself loosed from restraint, a convulsive effort of the tail drove the sickened, half-alive beast some five feet diagonally across the stream, and then it helplessly resigned itself to the force of the water, floating unresistingly down stream. Whether the good fish lived or died I know not; but, if it died—and many that have been hooked, and fought well, I know have died—it were better that it should have furnished food for human beings, than for the foul-feeding carrion-crow, or the slimy ravenous eel.

"Time passed on, and still found me a denizen of Brig End Pool. Fish came and went, and some tarried beside me, and some passed upward. The kelts, one and all, dropped down the stream by degrees, and by

the end of May not one was left. In August,
I found myself surrounded either by fish of my
own standing which had passed months in the
water, or fresh-run salmon, the early kelts of
the preceding year which had now returned
from the salt water.

"During my sojourn in the pool, many and
many a lure passed over me, and many times I
felt half inclined to seize the tempting bait, but
I always restrained myself; every rock, and
ripple, and cliff, and stream, reminded me of
the struggles of my first friend the kelt, or
some other doomed fish, for many a gallant
struggle was I witness to, between the fisherman and the credulous fish, the victim of his
perfidious art. Of these some escaped, but
the majority were, after more or less resistance, dragged ashore and killed. Of the
various wiles practised by those fortunates
who did escape, it may be interesting to make
some passing mention. One, I remember, a
grand fish of some eighteen pounds' weight, at
the first touch of the hook dashed with light-
ning speed down stream, turning neither to
the right nor to the left, running out a hundred
yards of line. The fisherman having neglected

to tie a knot at the end, there was nothing to stop it, and the great fish sailed away sea- wards, dragging in his wake two pounds' worth of excellent tackle. No doubt a few hours relieved him from the encumbrance, and his would-be captor paid not too dearly for a lesson he was unlikely to forget. One very extraordinary escape I witnessed was precisely analogous to my own when a smolt. The fish **was** hooked from the north or high shore; terrified apparently beyond the influence of instinct or reason, he dashed madly up the shelving bank on the opposite side, and lay gasping three feet beyond the shoal water. Taken aback **by** this utterly unexpected ma- nœuvre, the fisherman slackened his hold, and the fish, with the same effort that restored him to his native waters, shook the hook from out **of** his mouth. I have seen fish escape by running rapidly round a rock, obtaining either **for** themselves a dead pull, and so wrenching the barb from their jaws, or, leaving a dead pull against the rock itself to the fisherman, afford him an excellent opportunity of breaking his tackle and releasing his prey. I have seen a fish spring three feet out of the water, when

struck, and contrive in his descent to fall on
the line, so **as to** break the hold of the hook.
I have seen many, when but slightly hooked,
by a violent and continuous effort *shake* the
hook out of their mouths; and I have seen
others, well hooked but too tightly held, break
the strong line like pack-thread, or straighten
the hook itself as though it were made of pin-
wire. But perhaps the most efficacious, and
to the fisherman annoying mode of escape, was
one not uncommonly practised by a clean-run
vigorous fish. Indeed, I must own that,
though the kelts showed **more** craft and
cunning, and brought to their aid great
physical power, the fresh-run fish, for a clean
rush and a stand-up fight, beat them hollow.
The dodge they practised was as follows:
swimming near the surface, and rushing down
stream some thirty or forty yards, they suddenly sought the bottom, and returned upon
their tracks with scarce diminished speed. The
weighty water bagging out the line, gave the
fisher, more especially if a tyro, the idea that
his intended victim's course was still downwards, and, paying out line rapidly, he enabled
the fish to bring such a weight of water upon

it as eventually to necessitate its breakage. The first intimation Piscator had of the escape of his prey was the exulting bound of the salmon some fifty yards above the spot which in his imagination was **occupied** by that attached to his own line. This mode of effecting an escape I have heard designated as *drowning*, and **certainly I** have seen **fishermen,** after the manœuvre **had been** practised **at** their expense, look as though drowning were **an** enviable escape from their mortification. Another most successful manœuvre resorted to **by** a hooked fish, especially if a long line were **thrown, was the** running in **of the** salmon right **to the feet** of the fishermen. In vain the rod was held aloft, in vain the reel was wound with reckless **haste,** in vain its holder **receded** from the river bank ; **the** line *would* become slack, and a shake and **a** scuffle **at** once got rid **of the** hook, unless **it** had penetrated more than ordinarily deep, or **had struck** upon some **soft** part **of the** fish's mouth. Happily, however, for us, there are few such parts **in** our mouths ; if fresh-run **the** palate is soft, but **the** bone is hard beneath, and, **if** we have been long in the water, **it** is hard throughout; whether or no, a regular, firm, and equal strain must be kept on the hook, or the fish escapes; if the strain be too strong, the rod, or **the line, or the** gut, or the hook, or the hold in the mouth is broken; if it be slack, it is at once, and with ease, shaken out. On the whole, I wish we **had** no worse enemies than fishermen !"*

---

* I should think so ! In a water I once rented, I killed during six weeks, at an expense of a hundred pounds, forty fish, and was considered to have had good sport. Out of one pool on the same water, eighty **fish** have been taken at a single haul of the net !